This book belongs to

THE BABY'S BOOK OF

Baby

Animals

Kay Chorao

Dutton Children's Books
~ New York ~

For Jameson and Malcolm, with love

Every attempt has been made to trace the ownership of all copyrighted material and to secure
the necessary permissions to reprint these selections. In the event of any question arising as to the use of
any material, the editor and the publisher, while expressing regret for any inadvertent error, will be happy
to make the necessary correction in future printings.

The publisher gratefully acknowledges the right to reprint:

"My Little Sister," copyright © 1971 by William Wise.
First appeared in *All on a Summer Day*, published by Pantheon.
Reprinted by permission of Curtis Brown, Ltd.

"Grandpa Bear's Lullaby," copyright © 1980 by Jane Yolen.
First appeared in *Dragon Night and Other Lullabies*, published by Methuen.
Reprinted by permission of Curtis Brown, Ltd.

"Birthday Surprise" by Margaret Hillert. Used by permission of the author, who controls all rights.

"How a Puppy Grows" by Leroy F. Jackson. Reprinted by permission of Ruth W. Jackson,
from *The Jolly Jungle Picture Book*, published by Rand McNally, 1926.

CIP Data is available.

Published in the United States by Dutton Children's Books,
a division of Penguin Young Readers Group, 345 Hudson Street, New York, New York 10014
www.penguin.com
Designed by Irene Vandervoort

Manufactured in China   First Edition
ISBN 0-525-47199-5
1 3 5 7 9 10 8 6 4 2

~ Contents ~

A STAR DANCED

A star danced,
and under that
was I born.

~ *William Shakespeare*

WAKE UP, BABY

Wake up, baby, day's a-breaking,
Peas in the pot and a hoe-cake baking.

BOW, WOW, WOW

Bow, wow, wow,
Whose dog art thou?
Little Tom Tinker's dog,
Bow, wow, wow.

Bow wow wow

I'M DUSTY BILL

I'm Dusty Bill
From Vinegar Hill,
Never had a bath
And I never will.

HOW A PUPPY GROWS

I think it's very funny
The way a puppy grows—
A little on his wiggle-tail,
A little on his nose,
A little on his tummy
And a little on his ears;
I guess he'll be a dog all right
In half a dozen years.

~ *Leroy F. Jackson*

CHOOK, CHOOK, CHOOK

Chook, chook, chook, chook, chook,
Good morning, Mrs. Hen.
How many chickens have you got?
Madam, I've got ten.
Four of them are yellow,
And four of them are brown,
And two of them are speckled red,
The nicest in the town.

MY OLD HEN

I went down to my garden patch
To see if my old hen had hatched.
She'd hatched out her chickens and the peas were green.
She sat there a-pickin' on a tambourine.

CAN YOU TELL?

One is grey and one is black,
One's called Billy, one's called Jack;
"My two bunnies," said Miss Milly.
"Can you tell me which is Billy?"

"Though I must seem very silly,
I don't know, Miss, which is Billy;
Is he grey, or is he black?
Also, which of them is Jack?"

"Which is Billy? Who is black?
Who is grey? and which is Jack?"

~ *Ernest Nister*

MAMAS AND BABIES

"My Polly is so very good,
Belinda never cries;
My Baby often goes to sleep,
See how she shuts her eyes.

"Dear Miss Lemon tell me when
Belinda goes to school;
And what time does she go to bed?"
"Well, eight o'clock's the rule.

"But now and then, just for a treat,
I let her wait awhile;
You shake your head—why, wouldn't you?
Do look at Baby's smile!"

Kate Greenaway

THE ELEPHANT

The elephant carries a great big trunk;
He never packs it with clothes;
It has no lock and it has no key,
But he takes it wherever he goes.

SOMETHING ABOUT ME

There's something about me
That I'm knowing.
There's something about me
That isn't showing.

I'M GROWING!

WAY DOWN SOUTH

Way down South where bananas grow,
A grasshopper stepped on an elephant's toe.
The elephant said, with tears in his eyes,
"Pick on somebody your own size."

ANIMAL FRIENDS

Jenny loves her little calf,
   So gentle and so sweet.
Each morning Jenny gives her
   Sweet clover for a treat.

Amy's dog is not quite as good;
   He chases the hens away.
And now Amy and her doggie
   Must sit inside, not play.

∼ Ernest Nister

BOW WOW

ONE LITTLE DUCK

One little duck with a feather
On his back,
He led the others with a

quack,

quack,

quack.

Bow wow wow

Quack
Quack
Quack

FROM THE THREE LITTLE PIGS

A jolly old sow once lived in a sty,
And three little piggies had she,
And she waddled about saying "Umph! umph! umph!"
While the little ones said "Wee! wee!"

~ Alfred Scott Gatty

PIGGY'S BATH

Piggy, dear, don't squirm and cry.
The soap may run into your eye.
    Stop fretting, dear, no need for tears.
I'm almost finished with your ears.
    I promise not to scrub too hard—
It's only mud from our backyard.

~ N. Luka

HUSH-A-BYE, BABY

Hush-a-bye, baby,
They're gone to milk,
Lady and milkmaid all in silk,
Lady goes softly, maid goes slow,
Round again,
Round again,
Round they go.

MABEL, MABEL

Mabel, Mabel,
Strong and able,
Get your elbows
Off the table.

MY LITTLE SISTER

My little sister
Likes to eat.
But when she does
She's not too neat.
The trouble is
She doesn't know
Exactly where
The food should go!

~ *William Wise*

FROM THE KITTEN AND FALLING LEAVES

See the kitten on the wall,
Sporting with the leaves that fall,
Withered leaves—one—two—and three—
From the lofty elder-tree!
Through the calm and frosty air
Of this morning bright and fair.

~ *William Wordsworth*

PUSSY CAT MOLE

Pussy cat Mole jumped over a coal
And in her best petticoat burnt a great hole.
Poor Pussy's weeping, she'll have no more milk
Until her best petticoat's mended with silk.

THE CHILD AND MISS PUSSY

The child and Miss Pussy
Do play very nice,
But Pussy had much rather
Play with some mice.

THREE LITTLE KITTENS

Three little kittens
They lost their mittens,
And they began to cry,
Oh! Mother dear,
We greatly fear
   Our mittens we have lost.

What! Lost your mittens!
You naughty kittens!
Then you shall have no pie.
Mee-ow, mee-ow, mee-ow.
No, you shall have no pie.

The three little kittens
They found their mittens,
And they began to cry,
Oh! Mother dear,
See here, see here,
   Our mittens we have found.

Put on your mittens,
You silly kittens,
And you shall have some pie.
Purr, purr, purr.
Oh, let us have some pie.

The three little kittens
Put on their mittens
And soon ate up the pie.
Oh! Mother dear,
We greatly fear
   Our mittens we have soiled.

What! Soiled your mittens!
You naughty kittens!
Then they began to sigh.
Mee-ow, mee-ow, mee-ow.
Then they began to sigh.

The three little kittens
They washed their mittens
And hung them out to dry.
Oh! Mother dear,
Do you not hear,
   Our mittens we have washed.

What! Washed your mittens!
Then you're good kittens,
But I smell a rat close by.
Mee-ow, mee-ow, mee-ow.
We smell a rat close by.

THE SQUIRREL

Whisky, frisky,
Hippity hop,
Up he goes
To the treetop!

Whirly, twirly,
Round and round,
Down he scampers
To the ground.

Furly, curly,
What a tail!
Tall as a feather,
Broad as a sail!

Where's his supper?
In the shell,
Snappity, crackity,
Out it fell!

CRADLE SONG

What does little birdie say
In her nest at peep of day?
Let me fly, says little birdie,
Mother, let me fly away.
Birdie, rest a little longer,
Till the little wings are stronger;
So she rests a little longer,
Then she flies away.

What does little baby say,
In her bed at peep of day?
Baby says, like little birdie,
Let me rise and fly away.
Baby, sleep a little longer,
Till the little limbs are stronger;
If she sleeps a little longer,
Baby too shall fly away.

~ *Alfred, Lord Tennyson*

From THE LAMB

Little lamb, who made thee?
   Dost thou know who made thee?
Gave thee life, and bid thee feed
By the stream and o'er the mead;
Gave thee clothing of delight,
Softest clothing, woolly, bright;
Gave thee such a tender voice,
Making all the vales rejoice?
   Little lamb, who made thee?
   Dost thou know who made thee?

∼ William Blake

BAA, BAA, BLACK SHEEP

Baa, baa, black sheep,
Have you any wool?
Yes, sir, yes, sir,
Three bags full.
One for my master
And one for my dame,
And one for the little boy
Who lives down the lane.

BIRTHDAY SURPRISE

My birthday came, and in a box
That I got from my brother,
I found another little box,
And in THAT box, another.
And there inside the smallest one—
Oh, hurry, hurry, HURRY—
I found a little baby mouse,
All soft and warm and furry.

~ Margaret Hillert

THE MOUSE'S LULLABY

Oh, rock-a-by, baby mouse, rock-a-by, so!
When baby's asleep to the baker's I'll go,
And while he's not looking I'll pop from a hole,
And bring to my baby a fresh penny roll.

꙳ *Palmer Cox*

THREE YOUNG RATS

Three young rats with black felt hats,
Three young ducks with white straw flats,
Three young dogs with curling tails,
Three young cats with demi-veils,
Went out to walk with two young pigs
In satin vests and sorrel wigs.
But suddenly it chanced to rain
And so they all went home again.

Cock-a-doodle-do

Row row row my boat

Roar-roar

THE LITTLE BLACK DOG

The little black dog ran round the house,
And set the bull a roaring,
And drove the monkey in the boat,
Who set the oars a rowing,
And scared the cock upon the rock,
Who cracked his throat with crowing.

Bow Wow

POLAR BEAR COAT

Polar bear,
Polar bear,
That's a wintery
Coat you wear.

Thick and warm,
It must be nice
For playing when
There's snow and ice.
While winter winds
Flow wild and free,
I'd like a coat like yours
For me!

GRANDPA BEAR'S LULLABY

The night is long
But fur is deep.
You will be warm
In winter sleep.

The food is gone
But dreams are sweet
And they will be
Your winter meat.

The cave is dark
But dreams are bright
And they will serve
As winter light.

Sleep, my little cubs, sleep.

Jane Yolen

TEDDY BEAR, TEDDY BEAR

Teddy Bear, Teddy Bear,
Go upstairs.
Teddy Bear, Teddy Bear,
Say your prayers.
Teddy Bear, Teddy Bear,
Turn out the light.
Teddy Bear, Teddy Bear,
Say good night.

Good night

THE EVENING IS COMING

The evening is coming.
The sun sinks to rest.
The birds are all flying
straight home to their nests.
"Caw, caw," says the crow
as he flies overhead.
It's time little children
were going to bed.

Here comes the pony.
His work is all done.
Down through the meadow
he takes a good run.
Up go his heels,
and down goes his head.
It's time little children
were going to bed.

I SEE THE MOON

I see the moon
And the moon sees me;
God bless the moon,
And God bless me.